AN AMISH ADOPTION

BETH WISEMAN

COPYRIGHT

Elizabeth Wiseman Mackey
P.O. Box 326
Fayetteville, TX 78940

ACCLAIM FOR BETH WISEMAN

Home All Along

"Beth Wiseman's novel will find a permanent home in every reader's heart as she spins comfort and prose into a stellar read of grace."

—Kelly Long, author of the Patch of Heaven series

Love Bears All Things

"Suggest to those seeking a more truthful, less saccharine portrayal of the trials of human life and the transformative growth and redemption that may occur as a result."

—Library Journal

Her Brother's Keeper

"Wiseman has created a series in which the

readers have a chance to peel back all the layers of the Amish secrets."

—*RT Book Reviews*, 4 1/2 stars and July 2015 Top Pick!

"Wiseman's new launch is edgier, taking on the tough issues of mental illness and suicide. Amish fiction fans seeking something a bit more thought-provoking and challenging than the usual fare will find this series debut a solid choice."

—*Library Journal*

The Promise

"The story of Mallory in *The Promise* uncovers the harsh reality American women can experience when they follow their hearts into a very different culture. Her story sheds light on how Islamic society is totally different from the Christian marriage covenant between one man and one woman. This novel is based on actual events, and Beth reached out to me during that time. It was heartbreaking to watch those real-life events unfolding. I salute the author's courage, persistence, and final triumph in writing a revealing and inspiring story."

—Nonie Darwish, author of *The Devil We Don't Know*, *Cruel and Usual Punishment*, and *Now They Call Me Infidel*

"*The Promise* is an only too realistic depiction of an American young woman motivated by the best humanitarian impulses and naïve trust facing instead betrayal, kidnapping, and life-threatening danger in Pakistan's lawless Pashtun tribal regions. But the story offers as well a reminder just as realistic that love and sacrifice are never wasted and that the hope of a loving heavenly Father is never absent in the most hopeless of situations."

—Jeanette Windle, author of *Veiled Freedom* (2010 ECPA Christian Book Award/Christy Award finalist), *Freedom's Stand* (2012 ECPA Christian Book Award/Carol Award finalist), and *Congo Dawn* (2013 Golden Scroll Novel of the Year)

The House that Love Built

"This sweet story with a hint of mystery is touching and emotional. Humor sprinkled throughout balances the occasional seriousness. The development of the love story is paced perfectly so that the reader gets a real sense of the characters."

—*RT Book Reviews*, 4 stars

"[*The House that Love Built*] is a warm, sweet tale of faith renewed and families restored."

—*BookPage*

Need You Now

"Wiseman, best known for her series of Amish novels, branches out into a wider world in this story of family, dependence, faith, and small-town Texas, offering a character for every reader to relate to . . . With an enjoyable cast of outside characters, *Need You Now* breaks the molds of small-town stereotypes. With issues ranging from special education and teen cutting to what makes a marriage strong, this is a compelling and worthy read."

—*Booklist*

"Wiseman gets to the heart of marriage and family interests in a way that will resonate with readers, with an intricately written plot featuring elements that seem to be ripped from current headlines. God provides hope for Wiseman's characters even in the most desperate situations."

—*RT Book Reviews*, 4 stars

"You may think you are familiar with Beth's wonderful story-telling gift but this is something new! This is a story that will stay with you for a long, long time. It's a story of hope when life seems hopeless. It's a story of how God can redeem the seemingly unredeemable. It's a message the Church, the world needs to hear."

—Sheila Walsh, author of *God Loves Broken People*

"Beth Wiseman tackles these difficult subjects with courage and grace. She reminds us that true healing can only come by being vulnerable and honest before our God who loves us more than anything."

—Deborah Bedford, bestselling author of *His Other Wife*, *A Rose by the Door*, and *The Penny* (coauthored with Joyce Meyer)

The Land of Canaan Novels

"Wiseman's voice is consistently compassionate and her words flow smoothly."

—*Publishers Weekly* review of *Seek Me with All Your Heart*

"Wiseman's third Land of Canaan novel overflows with romance, broken promises, a modern knight in shining armor, and hope at the end of the rainbow."

—*RT Book Reviews*

"In *Seek Me with All Your Heart*, Beth Wiseman offers readers a heartwarming story filled with complex characters and deep emotion. I instantly loved Emily, and eagerly turned each page, anxious to learn more about her past—and what future the Lord had in store for her."

—Shelley Shepard Gray, bestselling author of the Seasons of Sugarcreek series

"Wiseman has done it again! Beautifully compelling, *Seek Me with All Your Heart* is a heartwarming story of faith, family, and renewal. Her characters and descriptions are captivating, bringing the story to life with the turn of every page."

—Amy Clipston, bestselling author of *A Gift of Grace*

The Daughters of the Promise Novels

"Well-defined characters and story make for an enjoyable read."

—*RT Book Reviews* on *Plain Pursuit*

"A touching, heartwarming story. Wiseman does a particularly great job of dealing with shunning, a controversial Amish practice that seems cruel and unnecessary to outsiders . . . If you're a fan of Amish fiction, don't miss *Plain Pursuit*!"

—Kathleen Fuller, author of The Middlefield Family

GLOSSARY FOR AN AMISH ADOPTION

Aamen: Amen
boppli: baby
Deitsch: Dutch
Englisch: those who are not Amish; the English language
Gott: God
gut: good
haus: house
kinner: children
lieb: love
mamm: mom
mei: my
nee: no
Ordnung: written and unwritten rules in an Amish district

schweschder: sister
sohn: son
Wie bischt: How are you?
Ya: yes

CHAPTER 1

Emily stood next to her husband on shaky legs as they peered out their living room window, each with a hand to their forehead, blocking the setting sun.

"He's smaller than I thought he would be." Dylan was cheek to cheek with Emily, the curtain parted barely enough for them to see the Amish woman and boy step out of the black buggy. "Should I go help her tether the horse to the fencepost?"

Emily shook her head. "No, she's done it hundreds of times, I'm sure. She'll be done by the time you get to the street." Dylan quickly put the curtain back in place when Caroline Yoder and Noah Jansen started up the sidewalk.

"I've only seen him twice." Emily bit her lip until it throbbed like her pulse. She and Dylan both stood on the other side of the front door, waiting for the woman and Emily's nephew to knock. "When he was born . . . and at Lauren's funeral."

Dylan put a shaky hand on Emily's back as they looked at each other wide-eyed, when the knock came. In less than a week, Emily had lost her sister and gained a child. She opened the door, forced a smile, and she and Dylan stepped aside so that Caroline and Noah could come in. The woman carried a small red suitcase.

A man from social services had called two days ago and asked if Emily and Dylan would be willing to provide foster care for Lauren's six-year-old son, then possibly adopt him. Emily and Dylan had fostered children before, so they were already registered and in the system. Although, the last time they fostered a child, they both agreed they wouldn't do it anymore. They grew too attached to each little person in their care. It was always a blessing when a child could return to a safe environment with their biological parents, but the emptiness for Emily and Dylan was almost too much to bear, and it often lasted for months. But this was different.

Emily and Dylan introduced themselves to Caroline, an Amish woman who looked to be about Emily's age, maybe mid-thirties. Emily had carefully planned what she would say in an effort to make the transition go as smoothly as possible, but she couldn't seem to find her voice. Even though she'd seen her nephew at the funeral, she'd been so distraught about her sister that she hadn't noticed how much Noah looked like his mother. The boy had Lauren's dark hair and eyes, but most telling was the shape of his mouth. Emily's sister had been blessed with full lips and a gorgeous smile. But Noah wasn't smiling. Emily reminded herself to be strong, not to cry over regrets, but to embrace this opportunity for her and Dylan to finally be parents. It was hard, though, since the tragedy of Lauren's death stayed with Emily like a dark cloud that hovered overhead everywhere she went.

After Dylan closed the door he took the suitcase and set it down. Emily leaned down until she was at eye level with her nephew.

"Hi, Noah." She cleared her throat, aware her voice was shaking. "I'm your Aunt Emily, your mother's sister." Nodding toward her husband, she said, "And that is your Uncle Dylan."

"*Wie bischt*," the boy said softly, his eyes cast downward below the traditional cropped bangs. He wore black slacks held up by suspenders, a blue short-sleeved shirt, and he held his straw hat by his side.

Caroline put a hand on Noah's shoulder.

"Remember what we talked about Noah? Use your *Englisch*." The woman waited until Emily stood up and she had both hers and Dylan's attention. "Children speak Pennsylvania *Deitsch* first. They don't start learning *Englisch* until they are five, so Noah tends to bounce back and forth between your language and the *Deitsch* dialect. We've told him to do his best, but to try to speak in *Englisch*."

School had just let out the day before. "We'll have lots of time to get to know each other over the summer."

Noah stared at his black shoes, one with an untied lace. Instinctively, Emily squatted down and began to tie his shoe, but before her hand even reached his foot, Noah stepped backward, turned to Caroline, and lifted his eyes to her. He spoke to her in their native dialect. Emily couldn't understand his words, but the emotion was clear. He didn't want to stay.

Caroline's bottom lip trembled as she blinked her eyes, moist with tears that threatened to spill at any moment. "You are going to be fine, *mei* little man. And I will visit as often as I can." She looked up at Dylan and Emily. "As long as that's okay with your new parents."

New parents. Now, it was Emily who might not

be able to hold back her tears. She dabbed at one eye as she nodded.

"Of course. Come visit any time." Dylan pointed over his shoulder to a platter of cookies Emily had laid out on the coffee table. "Noah, do you want a cookie?"

But the child didn't even turn around, only clung to Caroline's black apron.

"We've talked to Noah about this, but it will take some time for him to adjust."

"Don't leave me." Emily's precious nephew threw his tiny arms around Caroline. "Please, please." His cries grew louder, and as a tear slipped down Caroline's cheek, she pulled Noah close.

"*Mei* sweet boy, I will be by to see you very soon." She tried to ease Noah away, but he only held onto Caroline even more, sobbing.

Emily wondered what the relationship was between Caroline and Noah. All she'd been told was that an Amish woman would be delivering Emily's nephew today.

"You must stay with these nice people." Caroline tried again to detach herself from Noah, but he wailed. "You will just have to take him," she said to Dylan.

Emily had a hand over her mouth as she blinked

back tears and turned to face her husband. Dylan had a hand on his forehead as he took a deep breath. But he didn't move, his feet seemingly rooted to the floor.

Dylan finally put a hand on the child's back, but Noah screamed even louder.

Stupid, stupid. Why didn't they foresee this? As Lauren's only living relatives—with the exception of Noah's unknown father—Emily had thought Noah would want to live with them. Why didn't she think about him being close to other Amish people?

"Please," Caroline said to Dylan with pleading eyes and tears that streamed down her face.

"How will we reach you?" Emily had lived in Montgomery long enough to know most of the Plain people didn't use a phone. There were exceptions for business purposes and emergencies, but avoiding landlines and mobile devices was the general rule.

"This is *mei* address." Caroline handed Emily a crumpled up piece of paper she had in her hand. Sniffling, she still had a hand on Noah's head and spoke loudly above his cries. "It is always suitable to write to me, but you can be at our *haus* in ten minutes by car."

Emily took the small slip of paper as she swiped away a tear.

Dylan's eyes were moist as he tried to reach for Noah, but he hesitated.

"Please, take him," Caroline said barely above a whisper. Then she forcefully grabbed the boy's arms and held him away from her enough that Dylan was able to wrap his arms around his waist.

Noah kicked and screamed as Dylan carried him away from the entryway, through the living room, and toward the kitchen.

Caroline wept openly. Emily wanted to hug her, but some of the Amish were funny about affection. Instead, she continued to wipe away her own tears.

She opened her mouth to ask what the relationship was between Caroline and Noah, but Caroline spoke up first.

"Take care of him." Then she spun around, opened the door, and rushed down the sidewalk.

Emily took a couple of steps to follow the woman but stopped. She bent at the waist, put her hands on her knees, and tried to corral her own emotions as Noah continued to wail inside.

Caroline's hands shook as she flicked the reins and set her horse in a steady trot. She would cry all the way home, then put on a happy face for Abraham. At least she'd try to. Her husband was hurting as much as Caroline.

If there was one saving grace in all of this, at least Emily and Dylan lived out in the country. Maybe they raised chickens, or pigs, or had a pet of any kind. Caroline wished she had asked since Noah loves animals.

By the time she got home, Caroline should have been all cried out, but when she saw Abraham standing on the front porch, she exited the buggy, loosely tethered her horse, then ran across the yard. Disregarding all of her predetermined notions, she hurried up the steps and into her husband's arms.

"It was horrible." Caroline grabbed his suspenders as she buried her face against his chest and sobbed. "He screamed and screamed, and finally the *Englisch* man had to pry Noah off of me." She looked up at her husband whose eyes were filled with emotion. "Lauren would have wanted us to have him. She was my best friend, and she didn't have a relationship with her *schweschder*."

"*Ya*, I know." Abraham held her, rubbing her back. "But the law sides with family members."

Caroline stepped back from her husband. "*We* are her family. We've been around Noah since he was born. Lauren's sister showed up at the hospital to see Noah when he arrived, then not again until the funeral. "That's *not* family, Abe." She shook her head, which only caused her temples to throb even more. "If Lauren had been sick, and not died suddenly, she would have made plans for Noah, and she would have wanted for him to be raised here, by us, and grow up in the faith Lauren wanted for him."

Abraham ran his hand the length of his beard, which reached almost to the middle of his chest. They'd been married fourteen years, but God hadn't blessed them with any children. Caroline's stomach cramped up every time she thought about Lauren and the horrible buggy accident that had killed her instantly. But leaving Noah with strangers was shredding her insides.

"We talked to the social worker, and the *Englisch* couple—Noah's aunt and uncle—they haven't been able to have *kinner* either. And they have lots of experience, apparently, since they've taken in and cared for a lot of little ones."

Caroline folded her arms across her chest and looked down. "They don't have experience with Noah. They don't know him." She covered her face, shaking her head. "He's in an unfamiliar world he won't understand."

Abraham wrapped an arm around Caroline and led her into the house. She walked to the counter and eyed the box that she'd forgotten to take to Noah's new parents. It contained his favorite books, the cup he liked, a plastic horse, and a few other toys Caroline had brought from Noah's house. A new couple in the district was already interested in buying the place. Things were moving too quickly for Caroline, and as she put a hand across her stomach, it grumbled. She hadn't eaten today.

Her husband poured a cup of coffee and handed it to her. "Here *mei lieb*."

She took a sip of the hot beverage and set the cup down on the counter. Another tear trickled down her cheek, but there wasn't anything else to be said. Noah would be living with his English aunt and uncle, and there wasn't anything she or Abraham could do about it.

The void in her heart and the emptiness in her womb had never felt heavier. She missed her friend so much it made her physically ill. And when she pictured Noah being pried from her body, screaming, she squeezed her eyes closed and tried to banish the memory. But his cries resounded over and over again, echoing in her mind until she thought she might collapse.

Caroline sat down at the kitchen table and held her head in her hands. Her husband pulled out the chair across from her and eased into it. His tired eyes drooped beneath his bushy eyebrows as he slid his suspenders over his shoulders, then sighed.

"Did you tell the *Englisch* woman about the problems Noah has at night?"

Caroline rubbed her eyes as she shook her head. "*Nee*. I was so upset. And Noah was screaming. I didn't think about it." She nodded to the box on the counter. "I forgot to take his box, and his medicine is in there."

Her husband frowned as he shook his head. "It will be a long night for the new parents."

Caroline hoped so. Maybe they would choose to send Noah back where he belonged.

CHAPTER 2

Emily hadn't asked what Noah liked to eat or if he was allergic to anything, so she had to assume that he didn't have any known allergies.

"Noah, do you like spaghetti?" Dylan sat across the table from the boy, and Emily held her breath as she stirred the noodles, looking over her shoulder in time to see Noah nod. It had taken over an hour to get him to stop crying after Caroline Yoder left.

"Emily makes the best spaghetti ever." Dylan glanced at Emily and winked at her. He was good with children. They'd had foster kids that weren't easy to manage, but Dylan was patient with all of them. He was a born father, and Emily was excited for them to finally have a chance to be parents. Noah wouldn't be leaving them like the other children they'd cared for. Emily and Dylan would see him graduate, hopefully have a career, and get married someday.

As she looked at Noah right now, you'd have thought he'd lost a dozen best friends. His dark eyes were swollen from crying, and his bottom lip trembled. But he hadn't lost a dozen best friends, only one and she was his mother. He'd been ripped from the only home he'd ever known, and both Dylan and Emily were sensitive to that. They'd fostered children who had been removed from their homes in the middle of the night. Some of those kids had adjusted, and others never did.

Emily put a plate of spaghetti in front of him and sat down. "Dig in," she said.

Noah closed his eyes and lowered his head.

"He's praying," Dylan said, barely above a whisper.

Emily lowered her head but kept one eye open. She and Dylan had tried to encourage a simple prayer before meals with their foster children, but it had slipped their mind this evening. Even though she and Dylan were not particularly religious and didn't attend church, they believed each child should have an opportunity to find his or her way when it came to a higher entity. Prayer before meals was their way of an introduction in that regard. God wasn't something Emily and Dylan talked about, but she should have known Noah would be religious. They were going to raise him as their son so that made the spiritual aspect a bit complicated, but she wanted to respect what Noah had been taught so far.

Sometimes Emily felt a presence, a voice in her head, something coaxing her to explore the possibility of a relationship with God. Whatever pull she felt also seemed out of reach. Not wanting to leave any stone unturned, she had prayed for God to bless them with a child of their own. The blessing had come with a price though.

Surprisingly, her nephew—soon to be son—ate all of his spaghetti, and afterward, bath time went smoothly as well. By the time she tucked Noah into bed, his eyelids were heavy. Since Emily and Dylan had fostered children before, one of their spare bedrooms was decorated for a child Noah's age. She'd kept the colors neutral for a boy or girl—and they'd had both over the years—and it was a cheerful room. The double bed was covered in a yellow comforter with teddy bears riding bicycles. There were stars on the ceiling that glowed at night. There was a toy box filled with various items that were safe for children three years old and older. Down the hallway, they had another bedroom that was more suited to preteens and teenagers, and they'd cared for a few children that age as well.

"Do you want me to read you a story?" Emily fought the yawn working its way up from her throat, but story time had helped her to bond with some of the other young children they'd kept.

Noah shook his head. Emily wanted to kiss him on the forehead or cup his cheek and tell him everything was going to be okay, but anything she said would be hollow words to him right now.

"Dylan and I are just next door in our bedroom. So, if you need anything, come and get us, okay?" It was way too soon for them to suggest he call them mommy and daddy, but just the thought of she and Dylan as parents caused her heart to swell. Although the emotion was tempered again by the price that had been paid for Emily and Dylan to have a child. Her sister's life. Emily cringed as she recalled the harsh words she and Lauren had the last time they talked to each other. She took a deep breath and forced the memories aside.

She placed a blue teddy bear in bed next to Noah and left a nightlight on in the corner. There was also a glass of water on the nightstand. When he yawned, Emily did too.

"How do you feel about pancakes in the morning?" Emily smiled, hoping to entice the tiniest bit of positive emotion from Noah, but he just nodded and maintained the blank look he'd had most of the evening.

"Sleep tight." She backed out of the room and blew him a kiss before she crossed the threshold.

"Did you leave the door open?" Dylan was atop the covers reading when Emily walked into their bedroom. He lowered the book to his lap. In the past, they'd taken turns tucking in young children, giving them some bonding time with each child. They'd been good foster parents. Emily hoped they would be even better parents.

"Yeah, I left it open, and the nightlight is on. He knows where the bathroom is, so I think he'll be okay for tonight." She slipped out of her robe and got into bed with her husband. "You can tell the poor kid is exhausted."

"It's been a long day." He reached over and found her hand, gave it a squeeze. "I can tell you're worn out too."

She fluffed her pillow, but instead of lying back, she scooted over and cuddled next to Dylan, finding the comfy nook between his neck and shoulder. There had been so much to do today that she hadn't allowed herself to think about Lauren. When memories had forged to the front of her mind, she'd forced them away. But now, all was quiet, and it was all she could think about. She was plagued with regret.

"Thinking about Lauren?" Dylan pulled her closer.

"Yeah." She heard the shakiness in her voice. "All these years, she's lived less than fifteen minutes from us, and I never visited her, or went to see Noah." She paused as her chest tightened. "We said awful things to each other the last time we spoke."

"Don't do that to yourself, Em. Lauren forbade you to come see her or Noah, and she never came to visit us."

"I should have tried harder, but I never forgave her for not coming home when mom died. Our mother had raised us by herself for most of our lives. Daddy was only twenty-four when he died. Lauren should have been at the funeral."

"Try not to look back." Dylan kissed her on the forehead. "Instead, we'll put our efforts into being the best parents we can."

As she looked up at Dylan, she thought about how lucky she was to be his wife. Her husband wasn't just handsome and kind, he was compassionate and genuine. "Have you noticed how everyone in my family dies young? My dad. And, then my mom was only fifty-one when she passed. And my sister was twenty-eight." She rolled onto her back. "Maybe I'll go young too."

"Don't say that."

She looked at Dylan. He didn't use that stern voice very often. "Sorry."

"And, you said yourself that when your mom died, Lauren was all messed up, doing drugs, running with the wrong people, and jobless most of the time."

"Yeah, she was, and I'm glad she got straightened out but did it have to be with the Amish? I mean, couldn't she have found another religion to help put her life back together again? The way the Amish choose to stay apart from everyone didn't help Lauren and me to mend our relationship. If anything, the Amish ways discouraged it."

"I don't know, but there's nothing you can do about any of it. All we can focus on is being good parents to Noah."

Emily turned onto her side, gazed into her husband's eyes, and smiled. "Do you know how much I love you?"

"I should. You've told me hundreds of times." He rolled his eyes before he turned on his side facing her. "I believe it's to the moon and back times infinity."

"Correct," she whispered before a tear slipped down her cheek. Dylan brushed it away with his thumb and ran a hand through her shoulder-length blonde hair.

"I know you loved Lauren, and she loved you. Over time, I think you would have worked things out."

"I don't know. I could have tried harder to have a relationship with her," she repeated. "But I could only take so many rejections, and . . ." She began to cry, really cry hard for the first time since her sister had died. "She'll never see her son grow up."

Dylan pulled her into his arms and held her. He let her lie there and cry, knowing that was what she needed right now.

Exhaustion and grief met up, and Emily dozed off in her husband's arms. She didn't know how long she'd been sleeping when she awoke to a loud voice. It wasn't a scream. It was just loud talking. She jabbed Dylan with her elbow.

"Wake up." She got out of bed and threw on her robe as she ran around the corner to Noah's room. "Noah!" She rushed into his empty bedroom before heading down the hallway, realizing the loud voice was coming from the living room.

Emily's nephew didn't turn around when she said his name several times. Two at a time, Noah pulled books from the shelf on one side of the television and tossed them on the floor. He spoke in the language he was most familiar with, and his voice was loud. Emily wasn't sure what to do.

"He's sleepwalking," Dylan whispered as he came up beside her. "Don't wake him up. We just need to guide him back to his room. Remember, like we did with Brian?"

Emily nodded. They'd only had one foster child who walked in his sleep, but there hadn't been any yelling or throwing things.

When Dylan approached Noah, he put a hand on his arm. "Let's go back to bed, Buddy." He tried to gently nudge the child, but Noah wiggled loose and went toward the kitchen. Emily and Dylan rushed after him. He went from drawer to drawer, opening and slamming each one. Emily had child-proofed the house years ago. There weren't any sharp objects in the drawers. Knives were kept up high in a cabinet.

"Noah, Sweetie. Let's go to bed." Emily reached for him, but he cried out, again speaking a language Emily didn't understand." She glanced at Dylan. When their sleepwalker—Brian—had walked in his sleep, they were able to gently guide him back to bed, then go back to sleep themselves.

Brian was ten when they fostered him for about three months. But he'd never had this type of outburst.

"Do you think this is normal?" Emily whispered to Dylan after Noah stopped opening drawers and began circling the kitchen table. "Or maybe it's because of the move, his mother. . ." She didn't even want to say the word, but 'died' would be forever associated with the mention of Noah's mother or in reference to Emily's sister.

Dylan shrugged but moved toward Noah. "Hey, Buddy. Let's go back to bed." He tried to latch onto Noah's hand, but he jerked away, then leaned against the kitchen wall so hard that the dishes in the nearby china cabinet rattled.

Emily held her breath as Noah's eyes widened. "Caroline?" He screamed the woman's name.

"He's awake," Dylan said in a whisper before he slowly moved toward the frightened six-year-old. He crouched down in front of him. "You're okay, Noah. Remember Caroline brought you to stay with us? You're safe here. Maybe you had a bad dream?"

Noah's eyes were still opened wide, but he had stopped talking loudly and moving around. Emily was tempted to reach for the cookie jar, but she hated to give him sugar at two in the morning.

After a minute or so, Noah yawned, and he let

Dylan pick him up. Noah even rested his head on Dylan's shoulder.

Emily followed them to Noah's bedroom. Dylan carefully laid him in the bed, and Emily pulled up the cover, then kissed him on the forehead.

After they tiptoed back to their bedroom, Emily said, "I wonder if he's ever done that before."

Dylan eased back into bed, yawning. "I don't know. Some kids sleepwalk, and most of them grow out of it."

"But I don't think most of them throw books, open doors, and run around the house." She paused as she got comfortable beside her husband again. "Did you see the look on his face when he woke up? He looked terrified."

"I got up once with Brian when he was sleepwalking, and he woke up. He looked scared, too, at first." Dylan got prone and moved closer to Emily until he had an arm draped across her.

She wondered how often her husband thought about ten-year-old Brian. Emily still thought about him all the time, even more than the other children they'd cared for. Brian had been raised by his grandmother since his parents were in jail for dealing drugs. The judge hadn't gone lightly on them. Even though Brian's grandmother was granted custody of the child, Emily always wondered if he had returned to a safe place and a loving environment. Ties were severed between foster children and their temporary parents. The social workers said it was for the best. Emily wasn't sure about that. She reminded herself that this was different, that she and Dylan would file the papers to start the adoption process. They wouldn't have to return Noah to anyone or ever worry if he was being properly cared for.

"We will be good parents to Noah," she said through a yawn. "I might not have been a good sister, but I will be a good mother to Lauren's son."

Dylan sighed. "Stop blaming yourself. Lauren is the one who chose to stay detached from anyone who isn't Amish," her husband reminded her again. "That's the way they live. They keep to themselves."

It was a conversation they'd had many times. Emily's youngest sister was living a life Emily and her mother didn't approve of before becoming involved with the Amish. After her mother died, Emily recalled Lauren telling her she was pregnant. Emily was angry with Lauren for not coming home in time for their mother's funeral. She'd been somewhere in Oklahoma at the time with one of her many boyfriends. But, equally as upsetting, was the fact that Lauren was pregnant.

Emily and Dylan had been trying for six years to have a child of their own with no luck. She squeezed her eyes closed as she recalled the terrible fight with her sister.

She'd heard through the grapevine, which was small in Montgomery, Indiana, that Emily had shacked up with the Amish. She probably didn't have anywhere else to go since Emily refused to let her live with her and Dylan. And now she was gone.

CHAPTER 3

Dylan was flipping pancakes as Emily set the table when there was a knock at the door around nine the following morning. She glanced at Noah seated at the table drinking orange juice.

"Be right back." She shuffled in her socks and robe to the front door, wondering who would be visiting so early on a Saturday. Friends and neighbors had inquired about meeting Noah, but they'd gently asked everyone to give them time alone for a short while. That way Noah could adjust to them as a family of three first.

She opened the door and startled. "Caroline."

The Amish woman held up a brown paper bag, and she held a box in the other. Lifting the bag, she said, "I forgot to give this to you yesterday." Her eyes were still swollen as if she'd had the same emotional night as Emily. "Sometimes Noah walks in his sleep, and this herbal remedy helps him." She lifted the box. "And these are a few of his favorite things."

Emily nodded as she took the bag and the box. "Yes, we had quite a night. We've had sleepwalkers in our care before, but nothing like last night."

"I'm sorry." Caroline lowered her head, and it was impossible not to feel sorry for the woman. "I should have told you." She looked around Emily, who stood just inside the door. "Is Noah all right? I thought maybe I could just tell him hello."

Emily stepped over the threshold and pulled the door closed behind her. She took a deep breath. "Caroline, I can tell you care a great deal for Noah. But I'm not sure that seeing him right now is a good idea. I'm afraid we'll have another scene like yesterday. And, right now, we're trying to make him feel safe and loved. I know we said to visit anytime, but maybe we can hold off on a visit for now, until Noah gets used to us."

Caroline lowered her head again but nodded before she looked up at Emily. "Of course. You're right. He's just been such a huge part of our lives since he was born, mine and Abraham's, *mei* husband."

Emily could feel the emotion radiating from this

Amish woman she didn't know. "Can I ask how it is that you are so close to Noah?"

Caroline reached for a tissue in her apron pocket, then dabbed at her eyes. "Lauren was *mei* best friend. When she showed up in our community, she was quite a mess. Homeless, pregnant, and lost. The Troyers found her sleeping in their barn. We had the most room at our house since we don't have any children." She paused to clear her throat. "We took her in and tended to her while she was pregnant. She lived with us until Noah was born, then they both were with us until Lauren was able to get a job and a place of her own a few months later. I kept Noah during the days when Lauren worked." A slight smile lifted her expression. "We were so proud of her. She said she'd been at the bottom, but we were blessed to watch her rise to the top. It wasn't long before she chose to be baptized into our faith. She never married, but she was a *gut mudder* to Noah."

Emily could feel her emotions bubbling to the surface, swirling together in a tornado of confusion. Regrets suffocated her, and she was tempted to let Caroline come in and see Noah, to relieve some of the pain the woman was feeling. But, as Noah's mother now, she wanted to do what was best for him.

Emily also wanted to know more about Lauren, but that would need to come later too.

"There are a lot of things I'd like to know about my sister." Emily looked past Caroline as her thoughts continued to skew and collide. "And I know this is an extremely difficult situation for Noah . . ." She paused, rubbing her forehead. "I just think that we need this time, just Noah, my husband, and me, to establish a solid foundation for Noah. We know how big of a change this is for him, and how hard it must be for you." Emily swallowed hard. "We want Noah to have a relationship with you and your husband, but we want him to recognize that we will be his parents."

Caroline nodded, her eyes cast down for a few moments before she looked at Emily. "*Ya*, I understand. I just . . ." She blotted her eyes. "I just don't want him to forget us." After shrugging, she let the tears flow. "Or maybe he should forget us. Maybe that would be best for Noah."

Emily's chest was tight as she blinked back tears. "I won't let that happen." She made the statement with a conviction she planned to honor. She recalled how she felt every time one of their foster children had left. "I promise," she said barely above a whisper.

Caroline nodded, then turned to leave.

Emily watched her walk down the sidewalk to

her horse and buggy as she tried to envision her sister living that type of life.

After she went back into the house, she dried her eyes and started back to the kitchen, but went into her bedroom instead. As much as she'd like to give Noah the box with his favorite things, he would know it had been Caroline at the door. She could pass off the medication like she'd forgotten to give it to him last night.

Dylan was flipping the pancakes high in the air and failing miserably when she entered the kitchen. As one of the flapjacks landed in the sink, Noah laughed, and it was more than just music to Emily's ears, it was the sound of family. There had been a lot of laughter in the room over the years, and she and Dylan had been grateful for the opportunity to provide relief for children in need. But they'd always known it was temporary. This wasn't, and it felt wonderfully different.

Noah sat at a chair at the table, his expression bright. Emily touched him on the shoulder as she made her way to her husband. "He isn't a very good pancake flipper, is he?"

The child shook his head, grinning. "*Nee*, not *gut* at all."

"Hey, now." Dylan flipped another pancake, this time catching it in the pan. "If you two want to eat, be nice to the cook." He glanced at Emily. "Who was at the door?"

She held up the bag before placing it on the counter. "A delivery. I'll explain later."

Noah giggled when Dylan missed the mark again, this time the pancake landed on the floor.

Emily sat down beside Noah. "Yuck, I'm not eating that one. Are you?"

Noah shook his head, and Emily thought her heart might burst with happiness as he held onto the smile. But she wasn't a hundred percent in the moment. Noah looked so much like Lauren that it was hard to push thoughts of her sister aside.

After the salvaged pancakes were on a plate in the middle of the table, next to a platter of bacon and bowl of scrambled eggs, Noah bowed his head.

Emily glanced at Dylan and they lowered their heads as well. Even though they'd often said prayers aloud with children in their care before, Emily found herself wondering what Noah was praying about. Was he thanking God for the food? Did he want God to send him back to Caroline's house?

She decided not to speculate, but to offer up her own prayers, which felt awkward since she hadn't ever prayed on a regular basis. But she'd never been in a role as crucial as this one. It wasn't a temporary situation. She would forever be a mother to Noah.

Dear God, I'm unworthy of the gift of this child You've sent to us, but I pray that Dylan and I will be the best parents we can be and that we will always make the best decisions for Noah. She paused when she thought she felt something deep inside, a feeling she didn't recognize, a type of warmth, an understanding. Was it God? Did He actually hear her? She'd had similar feelings before but was never sure. She lifted her head and locked eyes with Dylan, who smiled. Noah continued to pray.

When he finally looked up, Dylan said, "Let's eat!"

Emily helped Noah spread butter on his pancakes, and their new family member reached for two pieces of bacon. After they filled their plates and everyone was eating, Emily had one more prayer to silently say. *Thank you, God.*

Caroline fought tears all the way home, despite the sunshine and colorful foliage on either side of the road. The warm temperature of early summer mixed with the hint of a leftover spring breeze. There wasn't a cloud in the sky, but the clouds across Caroline's heart weren't going to lift any time soon.

Emily and her husband seemed like nice people.

Caroline knew that Lauren's relationship with her sister hadn't been good, and she was certain Lauren would have wanted Noah with her and Abraham, but the Lord's will was being done, and Caroline needed to accept it. If only her heart could get in sync with the logic of it all.

Abraham was washing his hands under the pump near the gate when Caroline pulled in. Sniffling, she did her best to wipe away her tears. Her husband was hurting, too, and seeing her cry would only make things worse for him.

He wiped his hands on his shirt and searched her eyes. "How was Noah?"

Caroline raised her chin and stood taller. "I didn't get to see him. Emily thought it would be best for Noah if they establish themselves as a family before he sees us." Despite all her efforts, her bottom lip began to quiver. "She's probably right," she said in a whisper, longing for comfort from her husband. Instead, his face turned red.

"Nothing is right about this situation. Noah should be with us." He turned away from her, and Caroline suspected it was to hide his feelings. She walked up behind him and put her arms around him, resting her head against his back.

"I might be wrong, Abe, but I think Emily and her husband will allow us to have a place in Noah's life." She squeezed her eyes closed as she kept her head pressed against her husband.

"His place should be here." He slowly turned around, his eyes red with emotion. "We don't even know if they are people of faith. Noah won't know the teachings of the *Ordnung*. Do they even go to church?"

Caroline cupped her husband's cheek as his eyes watered, along with her own. "We've talked about all of this, Abe. We have to trust the Lord's will." In reality, Caroline wanted to lash out at God, to scream, to go back and snatch Noah from the English. But she chose, instead, to offer comfort to her husband.

Abraham reached for her hand, then pressed it to his lips, kissing it tenderly. "I know."

They walked hand in hand across the front yard, up the porch steps, and into their quiet house. A place of great sorrow following Lauren's death. But then, there had been laughter as they'd tried to brighten Noah's days.

Now, it was just quiet.

"What's in the bag?" Dylan asked in a whisper as they cleared the breakfast dishes. Noah had gone to his bedroom, which Emily had stocked with everything a six-year-old might like.

"It was Caroline at the door, and she said it's herbs that helped Noah sleep without having nightmares." She sighed as she placed two plates in the dishwasher. "I feel sorry for her."

Dylan opened the small paper bag. "It looks like candy, round chocolate candy." He raised an eyebrow as he took one out and inspected it. "Are the herbs supposed to be inside? How do we know it's safe?"

Emily placed their forks in the dishwasher tray, then stood up and wiped her hands on a kitchen towel. "They love Noah. I don't think they'd do anything to harm him. They sent over a box with some of his favorite things, but I'll give that to him when he's better settled. He'd know Caroline was here."

"There's only six in the bag." Dylan dropped the round chocolate ball back into the bag.

"I guess that's her excuse to come back over, or for us to go to her for more, assuming it works." Emily recalled the sorrow etched across Caroline's face. "She wanted to see Noah, but I explained to her that we needed to establish ourselves as a family. I told her I worried we'd have another scene like before. I could tell she was disappointed, but she seemed to understand and want what's best for Noah."

"Six more days isn't enough time to establish a family unit." Dylan set the bag back on the counter. "I'll take one tonight before bed. I don't want to give Noah anything without trying it first."

"That might mean another night of sleepwalking, but I agree that one of us should probably try it first." She smiled a little. "And you're the one who has the most trouble falling asleep. Maybe Caroline will give us some extras for you if it works."

"Seems weird to give a kid chocolate right before bed." Dylan frowned. "I guess we give it to him, then he can brush his teeth. But I'll try one first."

"Should we go check on him?" Emily asked before they'd even finished cleaning the kitchen. "There are tons of toys in his room, but have you noticed that when I turn on the TV, he walks away? I figured he would be thrilled to have a television since the Amish don't allow it."

"Maybe he thinks he's breaking the rules if he watches it, even though we told him it was okay." Dylan motioned with his hand. "Let's go take a peek at him."

Emily followed her husband to their son's bedroom, tiptoeing in their socks until they were in the doorway. Emily brought a hand to her chest and bit her bottom lip. Noah had lifted the window and had his face pressed up against the screen. Two horses and buggies were going down the road. He'd arrived with his straw hat, and he had left it in his room. But he wore it now.

"Noah?" Dylan spoke softly. It took a few seconds for the child to turn around, and Emily's breath seized in her throat when he did. Tears rolled down his sweet face which was streaked red.

"I want to go home," he said, barely able to catch his breath.

Emily wanted to tell him that he was home, that he had two parents who would love him until the end of time. She slowly shuffled toward him and bent down. "Honey, everything is going to be okay," she whispered as she put a hand on his arm. He didn't jerk away from her, but he wouldn't look at her either.

"I want to go home," he said again, still struggling to catch his breath.

Emily glanced over her shoulder at Dylan still standing in the doorway, his face looking drawn, his expression one of pained confusion.

Finally, Noah turned to Emily. "*Mei* visit is over. I want to be home with *men mamm*."

Emily put her free hand on her stomach, right were the punch to the gut might as well have happened. "Sweetie, I know Caroline talked to you about your mommy, that she went to be with God. Right?"

Dylan walked to the other side of Noah and touched his head. "It makes us so happy to have you here," he said, trying to sound upbeat. "Do you think maybe you could stay a while longer? I know you miss your mom, but I think if you give it—"

"I want Caroline and Abraham!" This time Noah screamed so loud that Emily and Dylan both flinched before they locked eyes. They'd both been trained and experienced situations like this, but it hadn't hit so close to home before. This child was Emily's flesh and blood, her nephew at the very least. But as she stared at this terrified, screaming, unhappy child, Emily saw her sister.

She lowered her head and covered her face, knowing she wasn't handling things correctly at all. But it felt like someone was clawing at her insides, unearthing feelings she'd tried to avoid. She couldn't stop crying as she fell from her squatting position all the way to the floor.

"Hey, Buddy, why don't we go outside and watch for more buggies?" Dylan's voice was shaky, but Noah sucked in air, his cries becoming more of a whimper. "We have a lot of buggies go by on the dirt road."

Noah let Dylan pick him up. "Let's give Emily a few minutes to herself."

She was glad Dylan hadn't referred to her as mommy, a title she hadn't earned yet.

As she watched from the window, her husband carried Noah into the front yard and they sat down facing the street together.

Emily pulled her knees to her chest and wrapped her arms around herself, tears spilling onto her white robe. As upset as she was about Noah, there was an underlying pain so acute, she wondered if she was going to throw up.

I'm so sorry, Lauren. I'm sorry I didn't make more of an effort to help you, to get to know you in your new life, to have an opportunity while you were alive to love your son, to see you as a mommy . . . I'm sorry.

CHAPTER 4

Emily bolted straight up when she heard movement coming from Noah's bedroom. It sounded like he was opening and closing his dresser drawer. She nudged Dylan, who had fallen directly asleep after popping one of the chocolate balls in his mouth. Emily thought the herbs were supposed to stop sleepwalking, not sedate a person.

"Dylan!"

Emily didn't wait for her husband and rushed from her bedroom to Noah's, where he was indeed slamming the middle drawer of his dresser repeatedly.

She touched him on the arm. "Let's go back to bed, Noah," she whispered in the darkness. Only the light of the moon shone into the room, along with a nightlight in the corner.

When he kept slamming the drawers, she wondered how Dylan was sleeping through this. "Honey, let's don't do that," she said as she gently took hold of one of Noah's wrists. He jerked away, screamed, and ran into the wall, knocking himself down.

"Noah!"

Emily darted toward the light switch, flipped it on, then ran and picked him up. She could already see a goose egg forming on his forehead. As he began to flail and wiggle, she was about to drop him so she set him down. He backed away from her until he was up against the dresser.

"You're not *Mamm*! You're not *Mamm*!" he cried.

"No, baby, I'm not." Emily fought to keep from crying. Noah was awake and confused. "But I'm going to help you get tucked into bed, okay?"

He darted across the room to the far corner, like an animal being trapped, his eyes wild and searching hers.

"Noah, you're okay. Nothing is going to hurt you. You were dreaming, and now it's time to get back in bed." *Dylan, where are you?*

"I want Caroline." He flattened his palms against the walls on either side of him. "*Mamm* said you should let me live with Caroline."

Emily covered her face with her hands, but quickly lowered her arms. This wasn't a time to fall apart. She eased closer to Noah, and when he lowered his arms, relaxing a little, she walked all the way to him and once again scrunched down.

"You must have been dreaming about your mother. I bet that was nice, seeing her in your dreams." Emily wished she could see her sister in her dreams. Sometimes she saw her mother and others who had passed, but not Lauren. She reached up to touch Noah's forehead, to at least turn his head to have a better look at the growing knot, but he moved to the side and out of her reach. "I think we need to put some ice on your head. Can you come with me to the kitchen?" She forced a smile. "And I think maybe some cookies and milk are in order. What do you think?"

He stopped crying but merely stared at her. "*Mamm* said you should let me live with Caroline," he said again.

Emily lowered her head, planned out what she would say, then looked back at the tearful child in front of her. "I know you think that's what mommy said, but the best place for you to be is here. I'm your mother's sister. We grew up together, and . . ." Emily started to recall the ways she'd failed her younger sister, but she cleared her throat, determined to keep herself together.

"She also said she forgives you," Noah said softly.

Emily tensed. "What?"

"*Mamm* said she forgives you. And she said she wants you to forgive her." Noah's gaze met hers as a tear trickled down Emily's cheek.

With slow intent, Noah reached up and brushed away Emily's tear. She didn't move, just stared at this gorgeous boy her sister had been gifted, only for them to be parted much too soon.

It was unexpected when Noah wrapped his arms around Emily's neck, but it was such a gratifying gesture that Emily couldn't hold back her tears.

"Don't cry," Noah said softly as he patted her on the back.

"God, if you are there, I need some clarity," she said as she cried in Noah's arms. It was a role reversal and in the worst possible way. A six-year-old who'd recently lost his mother, and everything he'd ever known, was comforting her.

Noah leaned away from her and put a hand to his chest. "*Gott* is always right here. *Mamm* said that. Caroline says that too." His eyes watered up again. "Can I please go see Caroline and Abraham tomorrow?"

Emily stared at the beautiful child in front of her and nodded. "But only if you let me put some ice on your forehead and eat cookies with me."

Noah smiled. "*Ya*, okay."

The next morning Emily awoke early, her eyes swollen and sore. She rolled on to her side, and Dylan smiled. "Best night's sleep I've had in a long time." Then he noticed her eyes. "What's wrong?"

"Well, I'm not sure we should ever give those little chocolate balls to Noah. It was like you took a sleeping pill." After yawning, Emily filled him in on everything that happened. Somehow she managed to do it without crying.

"Em, it had to have been truly emotional for you, but do you think you should have agreed to take him to see Caroline and her husband? We were going to wait on that, get him stable here first, feeling like he belonged in our family."

She squeezed her eyes closed and sighed. "I know, I know, but I kept seeing Lauren's face blending with Noah's, and there was such great sadness. I just wanted to make him happy."

"You can't break your promise." He ran a hand through his hair. "I've got a lot to do today, even though it's Sunday, but I can hold off on some of it and go with you if you want."

Dylan was an architect with more clients than he could handle sometimes. He worked from home, which often meant seven days per week in some capacity.

"No, no. I'll go. If it's a setback, we'll have to deal with it." She yawned again. "They have church every other Sunday so they might not be home." She had mixed feelings about whether to hope for that. "But I want to talk to Caroline about Lauren too. It seems like I have a lot of unresolved feelings bubbling to the surface, and I guess I want to know more about my sister's life."

Dylan leaned closer and kissed her on the forehead before he pulled her into the nook of his arm, the place she felt safest. "You know, we are going to get through all this. We are going to be wonderful parents and give Noah a good life. It might be different than what he's used to. There will be more tears, I'm sure. But, between the two of us, we have enough love to give that child to last a lifetime." They were quiet for a while. "I know you've always had some unresolved issues about Lauren, but you never wanted to talk much about it. But, Em, she was a grownup making her own decisions."

"But I was her older sister. I knew where she

lived. I even knew she had a son." She buried her head against Dylan's chest. "I should have reached out to her."

He eased her away. "You *did.* And she didn't want anything to do with you."

"But she didn't want me in her life because I was so critical of the way she was living. She was wild when she first left home, then when she went to live with the Amish, I called them a cult and said awful things to her." A tear rolled down her cheek. "And now I can't tell her how sorry I am."

He kissed her forehead. "It sounds like maybe she knows."

Emily lifted her head and stared at her husband. They rarely talked about God, just enough to be good foster parents, encouraging the children to pray and be grateful. "Do you believe in God, Dylan? I mean, do you *truly* believe? Do you think there's even the slightest possibility that what Noah said could be true?"

He was quiet and still for several long moments. "Yeah, I believe."

"Then why don't we ever talk about it?" She scooted back a little and propped herself up on her elbow. "Do you pray?"

"Yes."

Wow. There was no hesitation at all.

"Do you?" he asked.

She pressed her lips together. "Probably not as much as I should. Mostly when I need something." She cringed, but then remembered giving thanks for Noah recently.

They both jumped and separated when there was a knock at the door.

"Come in," Dylan said.

Noah walked in dressed in the clothes he had arrived in—black slacks, a short-sleeved dark blue shirt, and he was wearing his suspenders and hat.

"Can we go see Caroline and Abraham now?"

Emily smiled. She couldn't help it. Noah's excitement about the trip spread from ear to ear. "Yes, but let's eat some breakfast first, okay?"

He nodded and skipped off toward the kitchen.

"This is probably a mistake," she said after he was out of earshot, "but he'll never trust me if I don't keep my promise."

As Emily rolled out of bed, a list of questions swam through her mind, things she wanted to ask Caroline about Lauren. Then she thought about how awful it was going to be dragging Noah back home, probably kicking and screaming.

"Just some eggs and bacon?" she asked as she slipped into her robe.

Dylan nodded.

Emily yawned all the way to the kitchen. Noah was already seated at the table, and Dylan joined them shortly.

Once everything was on the table, Noah lowered his head, and Emily and Dylan followed suit. Emily cleared her throat. "Noah?"

He looked up, and so did Dylan. "Noah, I know that you've always said your prayers quietly to yourself, but I was wondering if maybe you would like to say them out loud? It's our tradition to say prayers together, to thank God for our food and blessings." Emily felt the sting of the tiny lie since they actually only prayed aloud when they were fostering children.

Noah tipped his head to one said. "You mean say the words in my mind out loud?"

"If that's okay with you? Or maybe we can each say a prayer out loud. Do you want me to go first?"

There was a twinkle in Dylan's eyes before he winked at her, then Noah nodded.

Emily wanted to thank God for Noah, but sharing that aloud wouldn't be in Noah's best interest.

She rubbed her nose, shifted her weight in the chair, and finally said, "Um . . . dear Lord, we thank you for our food, for giving us a roof over our heads, and, uh . . . for loving us." She looked across the table at Dylan. "Do you want to go next?"

"Sure." He bowed his head and reached out his arms to hold Emily and Dylan's hands, something she couldn't recall him doing before, even when fostering. This truly was a family now, *their* family. "God, we thank you for the gift of family, for this food as the nourishment for our bodies, and for the many blessings you've bestowed on us. We pray for continued blessings for all those we love. Amen."

Emily smiled at her husband before she turned to Noah. The small boy lowered his head and closed his eyes. "Dear *Gott*, if you can't send back *mei mamm*, please let *mei* live with Caroline and Abraham. *Aamen*."

Noah looked up and reached for a slice of bacon as if he hadn't just gutted Emily with his words. Dylan lowered his head. Emily knew there would be times like this, she just didn't know how much it would hurt. But it would take time for Noah to feel like they were a real family.

Not much was said during the meal, and when Emily asked Noah if he wanted to watch television, he shook his head and went to his bedroom.

"I know he's going to throw a fit when it comes time to leave Caroline and Abraham's." Emily tightened the belt on her robe as she sighed.

Dylan had already started to clean the kitchen. "I got this, the dishes. But, I can go with you if you need me—"

"No." She tucked her hair behind her ears. "It's okay." She took a few steps toward the bedroom before she looked over her shoulder. "I might wish you'd have gone with me when the kicking and screaming starts at the end of our visit."

Dylan kept his head down as he loaded the dishwasher.

"Thanks for cleaning up," she said before she rounded the corner.

About forty-five minutes later, Emily and Noah were ready to leave, and Dylan was in his office laying out sketches of his current project .

"Okay, well, we're off," she said as she peeked inside the room, Noah by her side.

"Okay. Have fun, Noah. See you in a little while."

They both waited for a response, but Noah just scooted quickly toward the front door.

Caroline collected eggs, the way she did every morning, but now Noah wasn't by her side helping. He loved the chickens, even their ornery rooster who seemed to only tolerate Noah, and not anyone else.

She didn't look up when she heard a car turning on their road until the blue minivan pulled into their driveway. After she scooped up two more eggs, she closed the gate on the chicken coop and trudged across the front yard. She wasn't expecting anyone this morning, certainly no one English on a Sunday morning. Then a familiar little person emerged from the passenger door and sprinted toward her.

She set the basket down and held her arms wide as she ran toward him, swallowing him up in a giant bear hug and smothering him with kisses. "I'm so happy to see you!" Squeezing him tighter, she looked over his shoulder at Emily as the woman closed the car door and moved toward her. Her elation foundered as she wondered what was wrong. She eased Noah away, kissed him on the cheek, and noticed the bump on his forehead.

"Why don't you run into the *haus* and see Abraham. He's painting the mudroom."

Noah darted toward the farmhouse as Caroline folded her arms across her chest. "What happened to Noah's head?" Even though she'd tried not to sound accusatory, she heard the implication in her voice.

"He had another episode with sleepwalking. But he woke up and got startled, hitting his head on the wall." The woman was dressed in a colorful sundress filled with floral blooms, and her nails and lipstick matched the rose-colored pattern perfectly. It was hard to picture Noah living with her.

"Did you give him one of the chocolate balls?" Caroline scowled, knowing her voice probably reflected her attitude. "Without them, he won't sleep and will almost always get up during the night."

"I didn't want to give him anything we hadn't tested ourselves since it isn't something prescribed by a doctor." Emily's tone seemed to confirm that she'd taken the comments as a jab. "My husband took one, and it was as if he'd taken sleeping pills."

Caroline didn't want to owe this woman any explanations, but she took a deep breath and reminded herself that seeing Noah was at Emily's discretion. "Noah used to take a lesser amount of herbs inside, just enough to control the sleepwalking. But after Lauren died, the child was exhausted, but he couldn't go to sleep. I should have told you that. Hopefully, he won't need as strong a dose after a while, but I assure you they are safe. I will give you a list of ingredients and you can check with your *Englisch* doctor if you'd like."

Emily nodded, then pushed a pair of pink sunglasses up on her head. "Can we sit somewhere and talk?"

Caroline wished she'd leave so they could spend time with Noah, but she motioned to the two rocking chairs on the porch. After they both sat down, Caroline said, "I'm surprised you brought him to see us. When I stopped by yesterday, you didn't think it was a *gut* idea."

"I still don't." Emily leaned her head back against the high-backed wooden rocker and sighed. "But it was the only way I could get him to calm down during his episode, and I also wanted to talk to you."

Despite it all, Caroline wanted the transition to be the easiest it could be for Noah. "I'm happy to answer any questions you have about Noah."

Emily twisted in the chair to face Caroline. "Actually, I would like to talk to you about Lauren."

"What about?" Alarms went off for Caroline. She didn't want to betray her friend.

"Last night, after Noah woke up during his sleepwalking, he said he saw his mother in his dreams." She waited, as if for confirmation.

"And you don't believe him?" Noah had often said he saw his mother in his dreams. Caroline had mixed feelings about whether or not such things happened, or if Noah just wished it to be so.

She rubbed her temples. "I don't know what to believe, but he said something that I'm hoping you can explain." She lowered her hands to her lap. "He said that Lauren forgives me and that she wants me to forgive her too." Pausing, she rubbed her forehead. "I know I wasn't the best older sister, and I should have tried harder to have a relationship with Lauren and to get to know Noah. I have tremendous regrets about that now that she is gone." She bit her lip when it started to tremble. "But I'm not sure what she wants me to forgive her for?" She waved an arm around her. "For this? For becoming Amish? Or did she miss our relationship, even a little?" She dabbed at her eyes. "Forgive her for not attending our mother's funeral?"

Caroline needed to throw this woman a bone, even if she'd stolen the most precious part of hers and Abe's life. "Lauren had many regrets. In the beginning, it was about the life she'd led before she found a home here. But as she grew in her relationship with the Lord, she told me that she had regrets about you too. She wanted you to be in Noah's life, but she'd ousted you because you didn't agree with her way of life. And, even though we believe in separation from the outside world, you were still her family. She talked often of ways to make things right between the two of you. But when you went to see Noah in the hospital nursery, you didn't visit her. She took that as a strong no, that you didn't want to be in her life."

Emily was quiet, her eyes moist. She looked a lot like Lauren, and Noah favored them both. Caroline's eyes grew moist, mostly from missing Lauren, not because she had a tremendous amount of sympathy for Emily.

"I assumed the baby would be in the room with Lauren. When I asked a nurse about Lauren and the baby, she said the baby was in the nursery because they were monitoring his heart rate. She assured me Noah would be fine, but I went to the nursery to see him, then I chickened out about seeing Lauren. I should have visited her, but I didn't understand your way of life." She locked eyes with Caroline. "I still don't. But she was my sister."

"You don't have to understand our way of life any more than we have to understand yours. But we coexist in a world where we are free to practice our beliefs however we see fit." She held Emily's gaze. "Do you believe in *Gott*?"

The woman hesitated for longer than Caroline was comfortable with. "Yes, I do," she finally said. "But I don't really know Him. I mean, I pray, but . . ."

This was the worst part of Caroline's nightmare coming true, that Noah wouldn't have a solid faith-based rearing. But she bit her tongue.

"I've prayed so hard for God to give me and Dylan a baby. I've prayed for years. And we've been blessed with some wonderful children to care for during their times of need." She shook her head, her eyes still locked with Caroline's. "But why did He deny me a child all these years? Now, my sister is gone, and I have a child to raise, but it came with consequences, and I don't understand how God works."

Caroline was tempted to be honest with Emily, to tell her that her own faith had slipped due to all the praying she'd done over the years, begging for a child to love. But she chose not to. "We must accept *Gott's* will, whatever it might be." She cleared her throat before she stood up. "I'd like to spend time with Noah while I have a chance." Even though she didn't want to sound snarky, she knew she probably did.

Emily stood up too. "I have a few errands to run if you'd like for me to leave him here for a couple of hours."

Caroline put a hand to her chest. "*Ya, ya.* We would love that." She couldn't stop the smile that spread across her face.

"This really is going against what Dylan and I discussed, about letting Noah get used to us as a family unit before we allowed others into our circle." She hung her head, then looked back at Caroline. "He is going to scream and cry when I take him home with me, and it's going to be horrible."

Caroline lowered her eyes to the cool grass, wiggling her bare feet. "*Ya*, but we will return him to you as I know we are legally bound to do so." She looked up again. "But we will make this time we have with him special and do our best to encourage him to go with you without a fight."

Emily lowered her sunglasses. "Okay, I'll be back in a couple of hours."

After she left, Caroline eyed the buggy tethered outside the barn, then she looked at the trailer Abe used to carry large furniture deliveries, and she wondered just how far they could get with Noah. It was a silly thought. If they were going to kidnap Noah, they'd go by bus.

CHAPTER 5

Emily went to the bank, stopped for a fish sandwich, browsed in an Amish shop, then just drove around the area. Montgomery was quaint and definitely had a plentiful Amish population. There were lots of horses and buggies traveling the streets. Emily and Dylan had a Montgomery address but they lived on the outskirts of the main town.

She drove by a one-room schoolhouse and slowed down as she tried to picture Lauren living on a farm and Noah attending school only through the eighth grade. It felt surreal, and when she'd first found out about Lauren's living arrangements, she'd been angry. It seemed traitorous not to at least share her son with Emily. Looking back, Emily reminded herself that she could have tried harder, a thought that always led her back to regrets.

Now, it was time to go pick up Noah. She took deep breaths as she pulled into Caroline and Abraham's driveway. Emily would have to drag her son kicking and screaming back to a place he didn't consider home at all. Why should he? Her heart hurt just thinking about it. She sat in the car for a minute before she got out and went to the door. All the windows were open, so they had to know she was there.

A large man, maybe in his mid-thirties, answered the door. He had a friendly face, and when he smiled, his cheeks dimpled just above his beard.

"You must be Abraham." Emily extended her hand.

After he shook it, still smiling, he said, "Welcome to our home."

Emily was surprised by the warm welcome since Caroline hadn't exactly rolled out the red carpet.

When Emily walked into the living room, Caroline was on the floor with Noah building a tower out of blocks. It was impossible not to notice the way Caroline's expression fell from a sense of complete joy to instant despair when she saw Emily. Noah didn't even look up, preoccupied with keeping the blocks balanced.

"Wow. That's a great building," Emily said as she tried to sound excited, knowing what was coming.

Caroline stood up and brushed the wrinkles from her black apron. "*Danki* for letting him stay awhile." She glanced down at Noah so lovingly that Emily was tempted to leave the child there. But she couldn't. He was her flesh and blood, her son. He would adjust, and it was just going to take time.

"Noah, it's time for you to go." Abraham spoke firmly, but there was a sadness in his expression that also tugged at Emily's heart. When Noah didn't acknowledge Abraham, the man spoke up again. "*Sohn*, it's time for you to go home."

Noah didn't look up as he placed another block on the structure. "I am home."

Emily sighed. "I knew this would be a bad idea," she said in a whisper to Caroline.

The two women stared at each other, then glanced at Noah.

"Maybe if he could come once a week to visit? We could promise him that and give him something to look forward to, *ya*?" Caroline smiled a little. Emily didn't want him to look forward to coming here weekly. She wanted him to adjust to his own new home.

"He's got to get used to us, to his new family. I feel like weekly visits would just make that harder." She rubbed her forehead, biting her lip, as she and Caroline edged away from Noah. "And you know he isn't going to want to leave, so it's going to be emotional for both of us when he throws a fit."

Caroline folded her hands in front of her, a blank expression on her face before she turned to Noah. "Let's pick up these blocks. It's time for you to go home now, Noah."

Even though she was trying to be firm, there was a tremble in Caroline's voice.

In one vicious swoop, Noah swung his arm and knocked down all the blocks, then ran toward the door, stopping at the doorsill.

"You don't *lieb* me anymore, Caroline!" Then he turned to Caroline's husband. "And you don't *lieb* me, Abraham!"

Noah covered his face, and as Emily's throat began to close, she swallowed back tears.

Caroline lowered herself to Noah's level and spoke to him in Pennsylvania Dutch. Emily had no idea what she said, but Noah hugged Caroline, and then he went to Abraham and the man scooped him up, kissed him on the forehead, and set him down.

Noah slowly shuffled toward the car, not looking back as he walked to the car.

"Please tell me that you didn't promise him we would come back next week. This is my fault, today. I shouldn't have brought him here." Emily shook her head.

"We'd like to disagree if that's all right with you. We are very glad you brought him here today." Caroline raised her chin as she blinked back tears. "There are two holes in our hearts." She reached into her pocket and took out an envelope. "I struggled whether or not to show you this. It's very personal, and it was intended for my eyes only. But, in light of everything that is going on, I feel I should give it to you. It's a letter Lauren left for me when she moved out of our home to her own house. Perhaps this will help you understand your sister, the person she'd grown to be."

Emily hesitated but took the letter. She turned around when she heard a car door slam.

"He's angry with us," Caroline said. "Hopefully, over time . . ." She shook her head and left the room.

Abraham muffled a cough with his hand. "It is difficult for us, but *Gott* will see us through this. *Gott* doesn't make mistakes, so there is a lesson to be learned here for all involved. But, whatever it is, sometimes it takes great pain and loss to allow us the freedom to be happy."

Emily didn't have a clue what he meant, but she nodded and went to the car. Noah was already buckled up in the backseat. He didn't say a word on the way home.

Caroline lifted her head from where she'd had it buried in her pillow. She didn't want to talk, but when Abraham sat down on the bed, she knew he needed to talk. She sat up, blotted her eyes with a tissue, and waited for him to say something.

"The *Englisch* woman, she seems nice." He ran his hand the length of his beard, something he did when he was deep in thought. "And she seems to want what's best for Noah."

Caroline sat up and tucked one leg underneath her on the bed. "*Ya*, she and her husband seem nice. But they are not what is best for Noah. Lauren would have wanted him with us and for him to grow up practicing our ways." She found her husband's eyes. "You know that, Abe."

He lowered his head and sighed. "*Ya*, I'm just trying to make sense of it in a way that helps us accept what has happened is *Gott's* will." He scratched his cheek before he looked back at her. "What was the letter you gave her?"

Caroline laid a hand on her husband's leg. "Something Lauren wrote to me after she'd been baptized. I didn't show it to you because I felt it would be prideful." She blinked back tears as she recalled the letter. "She mostly thanked me for showing her the way to *Gott*. But we both know *Gott* led her to us. We only worked under His directive. And, *ya*, the letter was to me, but I know her words were intended for you too."

"You two had a special relationship, and I recognize that. I just always wanted Lauren and the boy to be happy." Abraham placed a hand on top of hers.

"And they were," she said with a weak smile. "And, now they're gone."

"I sense the *Englisch* woman will let us see Noah and have a place in his life. She doesn't appear heartless to me."

"But it won't be the same. He will grow up watching television and with all the influences of the outside world. He'll drive a car, go to parties, and be faced with more temptations than we can imagine." Caroline sniffled. "I can only pray he will make wise choices."

Abraham pulled her close to him and kissed her on the forehead. "That's all we can do, *mei lieb* . . . pray."

Emily walked beside a very sad little boy all the way to the front door. She was happy to smell the aroma of freshly baked cookies and grateful she had a husband who enjoyed cooking and baking.

"I smell cookies." She closed the door behind her, but instead of heading to the kitchen, Noah went directly to his bedroom and closed the door.

"Maybe things will be better after he starts school," Dylan said after Emily told him about the past few hours. "I thought it was good that school was already out. I thought it would give him a chance to get used to us. But maybe it would have been better if he had kids to be around."

"Maybe. I'll try to arrange some play dates with mothers who have children around his age." She set her purse on the counter, then slid into a chair at the kitchen table. "Are we doing the right thing, Dylan?"

"Of course. You're his only family." He sat down beside her.

She slowly turned to him. "Or are we just selfishly wanting a child of our own so bad that we are taking him away from everything that's familiar? No matter what, it's obvious Caroline and her husband love Noah. We don't even know him."

"But we will learn to know and love him, Babe. We will be wonderful parents."

There was a desperateness in her husband's voice, an emotion Emily felt as well. But the day had taken a toll on her. Then she remembered the letter

Caroline had given her. "I'm going to go change into some Capri pants and a T-shirt. I'll be back." She stood up and took her purse with her.

She sat down on her bed and pulled the letter from her bag with shaky hands. As she unfolded it, she wondered if she would feel better or worse after reading it. She also wondered why Caroline wanted to share it with her since she'd made it sound like it was very personal and only for Caroline to see.

Taking a deep breath, she read:

Dear Caroline,

It seems like I should be able to tell you all of this in person, but I'm afraid I won't convey my feelings as well verbally. I want to be sure you understand how I feel. As Noah and I pack up to leave your home—yours and Abe's—my mind wanders back to the person I used to be. I know Gott *led me to you. If not for your unselfish, loving ways, I don't know where Noah and I would have ended up. I was in such a bad way when we arrived. Little did I know that* Gott *had set me on a path that would lead to a journey of not only discovery but of redemption. But you were His instrument, Caroline. Without you, I'm not sure I would have made it. I would have botched up my life further and surely ruined Noah's. You taught me about true love, how to not only love others with all my heart but to trust in* Gott's *love in a way I'd never understood.*

I wish my sister could see the ways I have changed. I have drained the water under my bridge, but I fear Emily's reserve is still quite filled with bitterness. I pray for her every day. I thank you for stepping in as my sister, and I will never think of you as anything less. You and Abe are my family, and Noah and I are blessed to be able to say that.

Even though we are moving into our own home, we carry with us everything you have taught us. I'm so glad Noah will grow up in a community filled with love, faith, and family. My shortcomings brought us to you and Gott, *but without those painful steps on the wrong path, Noah might not have this blessed opportunity to be on the journey I know* Gott *chose for him.*

Love always,

Lauren, Your sister in Christ

Emily wasn't sure when she started crying, but when she looked up and saw Noah standing in the doorway, there was no hiding her tears.

He was still wearing his suspenders and straw hat, and his puzzled expression was one of tense worry and concern as he stepped closer to her.

"You're crying," he said when he stopped about a foot in front of her.

"Yeah, I am." She sniffled, not knowing how to

explain her feelings to a six-year-old. "But I will be okay."

"I'm sorry you're sad." He inched closer, his head tipped to one side as he frowned. "Did I make you cry?"

"No." She shook her head. "No, you didn't. You didn't do anything to make me cry."

As Noah stared at her, Lauren's words echoed in her mind. "Noah, I know that you love Caroline and Abraham very much. And I know you miss your mommy. But is there any way that you might be able to give us a chance at being your parents? Your mother was my sister, and Dylan and I want nothing more than to love you as our son for the rest of our lives."

His face shriveled up, and Emily worried he might cry, but he took a big breath and blew it out. "*Mei mamm* wants me to be with Caroline and Abe."

Emily pressed her lips together, wanting to shout out, "That's what Caroline told you to say." She couldn't wrap her mind around the possibility that Lauren spoke to her son in his dreams, not at his age anyway. Kids were resilient and over time, Noah would adjust and adapt to this new way of life.

"I know you might think that's what Mommy

would want, but I'm actually your family, your aunt. I want to raise you as if you were my very own son."

"I have a family." He spoke with maturity and calm that Emily didn't think she'd seen from a child his age. "I have Caroline and Abe, and I have Mattie and Chester, and Lloyd, David, Mary, Annie, Sarah, Marianne, Paul, Big Jim, and a lot of other people. I have a big family."

Emily was still trying to reconcile her own wants and needs, largely in contrast with her sister's letter and what Lauren wanted for her son.

As she gazed into Noah's eyes, he let her pull him into a hug. "I'm sorry you had to see me sad like this."

He laid his head on her shoulder. "It's okay. I'm sad too."

Emily thought her heart might crumble into pieces. As much as she wanted to honor her sister's wishes, selfishness won out.

I'm sorry, Noah. I can't give you up. Please grow to love us.

Then, as she mostly did in times of need, she begged God for Noah's love.

And keeping Noah away from Caroline and Abe was the only way that was going to happen.

~

Dinner that evening was somber, and despite Emily and Dylan's best efforts, Noah continued to look like he'd lost his best friend—or that his entire, very big family, had been stolen from him along with his mother.

Emily rubbed lotion on her hands as she and Dylan got settled in bed. Her husband had just finished reading Lauren's letter to Caroline.

"How do you know she wrote the letter?" he asked.

"I recognize her handwriting." She closed the lid on the lotion and set it on the nightstand, then found her way into Dylan's arms. "Noah is too young to know what's best for him. A year from now, he will have been in school, made friends, and settled into our way of life. Maybe he'll want to be in Cub Scouts, and we should probably join a church. It'll all work out."

When Dylan didn't say anything, she wiggled out of his hold and looked into his eyes. "Say something." Her heart pounded in her chest. Had Lauren's letter caused him to reconsider the adoption? "We're right to have him. He's family."

Dylan stayed quiet as the lines on his forehead creased.

"Dylan," she said in a whisper. "Lauren isn't

here, and we have to make the best decision for him. And *we* are best for him."

"You said we don't talk about God together. Maybe this is a time when we should. Are we doing the right thing in God's eyes?"

Emily bolted upright, her eyes burning with tears again. "Don't you do this. Don't you second-guess our only opportunity to have a child. We've tried and we've tried. And we'd loved so many children, and none of them were available for us to adopt." She crossed both hands over her heart. "We have enough love for a dozen children, and we're willing to bestow every ounce of it on that little boy. What if he is our only chance to be parents?"

Dylan's eyes watered. "Em . . ."

She covered her face with her hands and shook her head. "No, Dylan. No."

"It's not about us. It's about Noah," he said in a shaky voice.

"No, no, no." She spat the words at him as she violently shook her head before storming out of the room.

He is ours.

CHAPTER 6

Caroline sat on the porch steps hand feeding one of the chickens that escapes the coop most mornings. She didn't hear Abe coming up on her from the backyard.

"Fence is repaired," he said as he made his way to the water pump.

Caroline tossed the last of the birdseed she had in her hand then leaned back on her palms.

"It's been over three weeks, Abe," she said when he sat down on the porch step beside her. "I guess Noah is settling in with his new family."

Her husband put an arm around her, and they quietly stared out across the pasture as the sun continued to rise in the distance. "I know your heart hurts, *mei lieb*. Mine does too. But we have to accept *Gott's* plan for Noah."

"I know." Caroline had finally stopped crying a week ago, but she'd also closed the door to Noah's bedroom and hadn't gone back inside. If only she could close the hole in her heart. There was an emptiness she couldn't fill. "I know you're right, but we helped raise that child. He's been a part of our lives for over six years."

"I guess the letter you gave Emily didn't sway her decision about Noah."

"*Nee*, I guess not." Caroline had hoped it would convey what Lauren would have wanted for Noah. "I know the feeling of a hollow womb, and it tends to override what might be right or wrong." She paused, considering the circumstances. "But if I were to conceive right now, even though we've been told that is impossible, it would not change *mei* feelings for Noah at all. I wonder if Emily could say the same thing. She wants a child, at any expense. I know those feelings, but this is Noah's home."

Abraham sighed. "We need a project, something to keep our minds busy. I've finished all the furniture I had orders for, and most of the repairs around here have been taken care of. We both miss the laughter, the boy's giggles, and his wonder at the simplest of things." He shook his head. "We need to keep busy as we heal."

Caroline didn't have much interest in a new

project. She missed her best friend so much that it was a struggle just to get out of bed some mornings. And she felt like she'd failed Lauren even though she'd fought the English adoption system the best she'd known how.

She closed her eyes and silently prayed that Noah was happy.

Emily reached for Noah and Dylan's hand, and they each said their prayers aloud, the way they'd been doing for the past few weeks before every meal. And she'd found herself praying throughout the day. She and Dylan had also been praying aloud in bed before they went to sleep at night. Mostly Emily prayed that she'd feel some sort of peace. Thankfully, her husband didn't voice any doubts about Noah not staying with them, even though she was sure they were there.

Noah hadn't come around, and the child was miserable, despite the fact that they'd showered him with gifts—an above ground swimming pool, a small trampoline, a train set, and a host of other things that barely piqued his interest. He spent most days staring out the window hoping to catch sight of a buggy going by. Apparently, you couldn't buy a child's love. And Noah always prayed for Emily and Dylan to let him go home. It was the dagger in their hearts before the meal three times per day.

After several arguments, she and Dylan agreed not to take Noah to see Caroline and her husband. Dylan thought a visit would be good, but Emily didn't think so. She could tell that Noah's disposition was wearing on Dylan. He felt sorry for the boy and hated seeing him so unhappy. Emily convinced him that they just needed more time as a family.

"I need to go to Walmart in Bedford today." Emily dabbed her mouth with her napkin. We can get a jump on school supplies. Are you excited about starting school, Noah?" It was too soon to focus on school supplies, but she hoped maybe it would spark an interest for Noah.

He nodded, but with the enthusiasm of someone being taken to jail. Ever since he'd caught Emily crying and hugged her, he hadn't thrown any fits or cried in front of them. She wondered, though, how hard he was crying on the inside. It didn't seem healthy for a boy his age to withhold his emotions, and Noah seemed to be doing it so as not to upset her.

It was early afternoon by the time she and Noah left for Walmart. It had taken some coaxing to get him to tag along. She and Dylan had only been giving him half of the chocolate balls at night, which usually worked, and Noah slept soundly. But on those nights when he was up and roaming, they usually gave in the following night and gave him a whole one. Last night, Noah had stumbled around his room mumbling to himself, but Emily had gotten him back to bed fairly easily.

"We can walk through the toy section and you can pick something out," she told Noah after Emily had stood in line and picked up a prescription that the doctor said might help Noah to sleep better. Even though the pediatrician said the herbs inside the chocolate ball wouldn't hurt Noah, he felt there were other options for him.

As had become his way, Noah tried to smile and nodded. But as they approached the aisle with the toys, they came face to face with Caroline. Emily felt a surge of panic that was soon justified as Noah ran to her and threw his arms around her waist. After Caroline had smoothed back his hair and kissed him on the forehead over and over again, she finally looked at Emily. The Amish rarely showed any public emotion, but it hadn't mattered now.

Emily slowly approached them, still embracing.

"I-I told Noah he could pick out a toy." She swallowed the lump building in her throat. "It's nice to see you Caroline." It was a lie she'd have to ask forgiveness for later.

"Take me home, Caroline," Noah said as he pressed his face into her black apron.

There was a sorrow in Caroline's eyes that Emily could relate to. "You have a home now, Noah, with Emily and Dylan," Caroline said.

Emily could see the woman's soul, the pain mirroring her own. She knew it took everything Caroline had to say what she did.

"Please, Caroline, please." Noah was starting to cry and clinging to Caroline the same way he'd done on that first day.

As Caroline latched on to Noah's arms and began prying him away from her, he only held tighter. "Noah, please," she said as her voice quivered.

"Stop." Emily laid a hand across her stomach and took a deep breath. "Noah, would you like to spend the night with Caroline and Abraham tonight?" She tried to keep her voice level, but it cracked just the same.

Noah quickly spun around and blinked his tear-filled eyes. "*Ya*. Can I?"

"Yes," Emily said barely above a whisper. "I can

pick him up tomorrow afternoon, maybe around four, if you'd like." She locked eyes with Caroline.

"*Ya*, we'd like that very much." She leaned down to Noah. "*Sohn*, you can come and stay with us tonight, but tomorrow afternoon when Emily comes to pick you up, you will have to go without throwing a fit. Do you understand me?"

The word 'son' slid off of Caroline's tongue with an ease that brought forth a pain in Emily's chest. Noah nodded, his bright eyes twinkling as a smile filled his face. Emily, Dylan, and Noah had brief moments of joy, but Noah had never looked at her—not even once—the way he looked at Caroline now.

"Do you want to pick out a toy first?" Emily asked, but Noah quickly shook his head, keeping his eyes on Caroline.

"Wait here." Caroline pointed to the basket she was pushing before she walked closer to Emily. She put a hand on her arm. "Thank you for this," she said in a whisper. "We will do our very best to make the transition back to you as painless as possible tomorrow. We have missed him so much . . ." She brought a hand to her chest. For a moment Emily thought the woman might hug her, but she mouthed thank you again and went back to Noah.

Emily watched them walk away, both smiling and laughing. After they rounded the corner, Emily took the prescription she'd paid for out of the basket and stuffed it in her purse. She left the basket in the middle of the aisle, then left.

Caroline refused to focus on the fact that Noah would have to leave tomorrow. Instead, she was going to enjoy every moment with him.

"Look who I have!" she yelled as she walked into the house.

Noah ran to Abe's arms, and Caroline's husband lifted him high in the air. "Do I know you?" he teased.

"It's me, Noah!" The boy laughed when Abe swung him in circles, his feet flailing around as giggles once again filled their house.

For the rest of the day, the night, and the following day, their lives were back to normal. The new normal, without Lauren, but the closer it came to four o'clock, the more Caroline's stomach churned. Would it always be like this? Could time heal them all, and would Noah settle in at his new home? Or would Caroline feel like her heart was being ripped out every time they had to return Noah to Emily and Dylan?

She brushed the thoughts away, resolved to make

each moment memorable, as the countdown to four o'clock continued.

Emily wrapped her arms around Dylan and kissed him on the cheek. "It will be awful. Are you sure you want to come?"

Her husband held her tightly. "Yeah. I don't want you going through that by yourself, and I should be there."

A half-hour later, they were in the car and on the way to Caroline and Abraham's. Neither one spoke, as if they were storing up energy for the emotional surge that was coming.

When they pulled into the driveway, Noah, Caroline, and Abraham were standing on the front porch, all with somber expressions. Emily was sure Noah had been given strict instructions not to fuss when they showed up, which tore at her heart again.

She stepped out of the car and met Dylan at the back of the minivan. She took out the small red suitcase Noah had shown up with. Dylan lifted out a larger one filled with some clothes and toys they'd gotten for Noah.

As they rounded the vehicle with the suitcases,

Caroline and Abraham's jaws dropped. Noah scratched his cheek.

Dylan shook Abraham's hand as Emily introduced the two men, but all eyes were on the suitcases.

"Will you be letting us keep Noah for a while longer?" Caroline spoke in a hopeful, yet cautious voice.

"Forever," Emily said as a tear rolled down her cheek. She'd reread her sister's letter a dozen times the night before. "I might have failed Lauren, but I'm not going to fail her son or stand in the way of what she wanted for Noah. I'll talk to the adoption agency tomorrow and recommend that you and Abe be allowed to adopt him."

Caroline clamped a hand over her mouth as her husband blinked back tears.

"*Danki*," Abraham said when Caroline didn't seem to have any words, her eyes as moist as Emily's.

"We will provide a *gut* life for him," Caroline said through her tears.

"I know you will." Emily looked down at Noah, who stared at her. She lowered herself to eye level with him. "I hope that you will allow us to be a part of your life, Noah. We wanted very much to be your parents." She glanced up at Caroline, then Abraham. "But, with your mother not here, I do believe she would want you to be with Caroline and Abraham." She lowered her head, trying desperately to gain control of her emotions. Dylan placed a hand on her shoulder before he squatted down also.

"But we'll still be your aunt and uncle, and I hope we will still have a place in your life."

Emily heard the shakiness in her husband's voice. He'd tried to be so strong for her the night before when they'd spent hours discussing Noah's future. But, now in the moment, he was struggling too.

When Emily glanced up at Noah, she was surprised when he laid a small hand against her cheek. "Don't be sad." Then he looked at Dylan. "Please don't be sad. I know I prayed to come home, but when I closed *mei* eyes at night in *mei* bed, I prayed that *Gott* would give you a *boppli* of your own."

"That means baby," Caroline said in a whisper.

Emily lowered her head again, fighting not to cry before she looked back at Noah. "I appreciate that Noah, but I don't think that's in God's plan for us."

With Dylan's help, Emily stood up, then she leaned down and kissed Noah on the cheek. The boy gently touched Emily's stomach and smiled. "*Mamm* said there is already a *boppli* in there."

Emily still wasn't sure she believed that Lauren

spoke to Noah in his dreams, but a burst of adrenaline shot through every vein in her body. She looked at Caroline, who smiled.

"He's usually right." Caroline put a hand on Noah's head.

"Well, if that ever happened, you'd have a cousin." Emily was sure Noah couldn't make a prediction like that.

"Stop by whenever you'd like," Abraham said as they said their goodbyes. "You will always be welcome here, and we want you to be a part of Noah's life. Lauren would want that too."

Emily wasn't so sure about the last part, and she forced herself not to look back as they walked to the car. She waited until they went around the corner before she let the rest of the tears come pouring out. Dylan was quiet.

She finally blew her nose. "We did the right thing."

"Yes, we did."

They were quiet for a while. "Em . . ."

She turned to him, sniffling.

"You threw up yesterday morning."

"Yeah, I think it was just nerves." She shook her head. "So hard," she said in a whisper. But then she caught the underlying meaning in Dylan's question and she pulled her phone from her purse. She scrolled to the calendar and counted backward. She glanced at Dylan.

"There's no way . . ." She smiled. "Is there?"

He shrugged. "I don't know. You're the one with the calendar."

Instead of turning right toward home, Dylan made a left. "Only one way to find out. Up for a trip to Walmart? I think there are little tests for things like this?" He winked at her.

Emily had taken dozens of pregnancy tests over the years, but as she laid her hand across her stomach, she wondered if this test might be different from the others. With everything going on, she hadn't realized that she was three weeks late for her period. She'd never been that late before.

They ran into Walmart with the excitement of children Noah's age, and even the checkout clerk grinned as they paid for two tests. If the first one was positive, she wanted a second test to confirm the results.

But on the way home, Emily's stomach began to churn. Doubt crept in like a deceitful old friend giving hope, only to stab you in the back with disappointment. Dylan had grown quiet also.

Two tests later, Emily threw her arms around her husband's neck. God had answered their prayers. Maybe it was because they did the right thing, returning Noah to Caroline and Abe. Or, had they reached the necessary quota of prayers that was pleasing to God?

Emily's conclusion was they hadn't been ready before. Noah had inadvertently shown Emily and Dylan how to have a relationship with God, and how to have a better relationship as a couple through prayer. She'd always heard that things happened on God's timeframe. And this was her and Dylan's time now.

Thank you, God.

EPILOGUE

One year later . . .

Emily carried a casserole as she stepped into Caroline and Abe's house. Noah almost knocked her over when he ran into the living room. But it wasn't to see Emily. After bumping into her, Noah went to Dylan, leaned down, and looked at Larna in the baby carrier. They'd named her after Lauren and Noah, and the name also meant peace or harmony, both of which Emily and Dylan had found.

"She's bigger than she was two weeks ago." Noah gently touched Larna on the cheek, which caused her to smile.

"She's three months old today," Dylan said proudly.

Emily went into the kitchen. "I'm not sure this cooked long enough. We might want to put it in for another thirty minutes." She set the chicken and rice casserole on the stove before she hugged Caroline. They'd been meeting every two weeks ever since they'd left Noah with Caroline and Abe. Emily never wanted to replace Lauren in Caroline's memories, but in many ways, the women had become like sisters, and she'd shared precious recollections about Lauren with Emily.

After Noah had returned to Caroline and Abe, Emily and Dylan had continued praying aloud before meals and at bedtime together. Emily still wondered if they would have found their more meaningful relationship with God if not for Noah. They'd eventually found a church to attend. She knew she had much to learn, but she also knew that you were never too old to seek Him out.

She often recalled what Lauren wrote in her letter . . . *My shortcomings brought us to you and* Gott, *but without those painful steps on the wrong path, Noah might not have this blessed opportunity to be on the journey I know* Gott *chose for him.*

Emily knew she'd been blessed as well—with Dylan, Larna, Noah, Caroline, and Abe. Something she never wanted to take for granted.

THANK YOU!

To my wonderful readers,

Thank you for reading *An Amish Adoption*. I hope you enjoyed this story as much as I enjoyed writing it.

Turn the page for some authentic Amish recipes!

Also, all of my books are listed in the back.

Deepest Appreciation,
Beth

AMISH RECIPES

Classic Amish Apple Pie

Streusel:

1/3 cup granulated sugar
1/4 cup brown sugar
6 tablespoon flour
1 teaspoon ground cinnamon
1 teaspoon grated nutmeg
1 pinch salt

Filling:

1/2 cup (1 stick) butter, cold
1/2 cup walnuts or pecans, coarsely chopped
1 unbaked 10 inch pie shell
4 large Granny Smith apples, peeled & sliced, about 4 cups

7 tablespoons flour
1 cup granulated sugar
1/2 teaspoon cinnamon
1 egg
1 cup heavy whipping cream
1 teaspoon vanilla extract

Instructions:

In a bowl, mix the streusel ingredients, 1/3 cup sugar, 1/4 cup brown sugar, 6 tablespoons flour, 1 teaspoon cinnamon, nutmeg and salt.

Add the butter and cut with two knives until the mixture is crumbly; it should still have a dry look to it. Add the nuts then set aside.

Preheat oven to 350 degrees F.

Place apples in the pie shell.

In a small bowl, mix 1 cup sugar, 7 tablespoons flour, and 1 teaspoon cinnamon. Beat the egg in a medium bowl, and add the cream and vanilla.

Add the sugar mixture to the egg mixture and blend. Pour over the apples.

Bake for 1 hour in the lower one-third of the oven. After 20 minutes, sprinkle streusel over the top and continue baking approximately 40 minutes longer, or until the top puffs and is golden brown.

Chicken and Rice Casserole

3 boneless chicken breasts
1 ½ cups uncooked rice
½ cup chopped onion
3 T. butter or margarine
2 ½ cups water
1 tsp. salt
1 tsp. celery salt
¼ tsp. pepper
¼ tsp. paprika

Preheat oven to 350. Spray an 8 x 13-inch glass casserole dish with cooking spray and set aside. Saute rice and onions in butter until light brown, stirring constantly. Add water, salt, celery salt, pepper, and paprika, then mix well. Pour into casserole dish. Place chicken breasts on top of mixture. Cover tight with foil and cook for 1 hour and 30 minutes. When done, cut up chicken and mix with rice.

Chicken Noodle Soup

1 broiler/fryer chicken (3 to 4 lbs.) cut up

- 10 c. water
- 1 large carrot, sliced
- 1 large onion, sliced
- 1 celery rib, sliced
- 1 garlic clove, minced
- 1 bay leaf
- 1 t. dried thyme
- 1 t. salt
- ¼ t. pepper

Soup Ingredients:

- 2 large carrots, sliced
- 2 celery ribs, sliced
- 1 medium onion, chopped
- 2 c. egg noodles, uncooked
- 1 c. frozen peas
- ½ c. cut green beans, frozen

In a large soup kettle or Dutch oven, combine the first ten ingredients. Bring to a boil. Reduce heat; cover and simmer for 1 ½ to 2 hours or until the meat is tender.

Remove chicken and cool. Remove and discard skin and bones. Chop chicken and set aside. Strain broth, discarding vegetables and bay leaf. Return broth to the pan; add carrots, celery, and onion. Bring to a boil. Reduce heat; cover and simmer for 10 minutes or until the vegetables are tender.

Add noodles and chicken. Bring to a boil. Reduce heat; cover and simmer for 6 minutes. Stir in peas and beans. Cook for 2 to 4 minutes or until beans and noodles are tender. Yield: 6 to 8 servings.

Cinnamon Raisin Bread

2 c. warm water

2 packages (1/4 ounce each) active dry yeast

1 c. sugar, divided

¼ c. canola oil

2 tsp. salt

2 eggs

6 to 6 ½ c. all-purpose flour

1 c. raisins

Extra canola oil

3 tsp. ground cinnamon

Using a large bowl, dissolve yeast in warm water. Add ½ cup sugar, oil, salt, eggs, and 4 cups flour. Beat until smooth. Stir in enough remaining flour until it forms a soft dough.

On a floured surface; knead until smooth and elastic, about 6 to 8 minutes. Place in a greased bowl, turning once to grease top. Cover and let rise in a warm place or until doubled, about 1 hour.

Punch dough down. Turn onto a lightly floured surface; divide in half. Knead ½ cup raisins into each; roll each portion into a 15x9-in. rectangle. Brush with additional oil. Combine cinnamon and remaining sugar; sprinkle to within ½ in. of edges.

Tightly roll up, jelly-roll styled, starting with a short side; pinch seam to seal. Place, seam side down, in two greased 9x4-in. loaf pans. Cover and let rise until doubled, about 30 minutes.

Preheat oven to 375. Brush with oil. Bake 45-50 minutes or until golden brown. Remove from pans and cool on wire racks. Yield – 2 loaves (16 slices each).

Meat Pie

2 1/2 pounds potatoes. Peeled and cut in half inch squares

2 pounds boneless chuck roast

Salt

Pepper

2 uncooked pie crusts. (Recipe below or can use frozen)

Place chuck roast in Dutch oven or similar size pot.

Add water to cover. Bring to a boil. Continue simmering until tender. (2 to 3 hours)

Boil potatoes until soft (about 20 minutes). Drain.

Cut cooked roast in cubes and mix with potatoes.

Salt and pepper to taste

Fill uncooked pie crust and cover with top crust. Score top of crust to vent

Bake at 350 degrees for 45 minutes. Serve with brown gravy.

Pie crust (makes two)

3 cups all purpose flour

4 teaspoons white sugar

2 teaspoons salt

1 cup vegetable oil
4 tablespoons milk

Mix together in large mixing bowl. Divide in half. Chill for 1 hour. Roll each crust out on wax paper. (Sprinkle flour on top before rolling).

Paprika Potatoes

¼ cup flour
¼ cup Parmesan cheese
1 Tbsp. paprika
¾ tsp. salt
1/8 tsp. garlic salt (or onion salt)
6 medium potatoes
vegetable oil or cooking spray

Put all the ingredients, except the potatoes, into a gallon-size plastic baggie. Shake until well blended. Wash the potatoes and cut them into small wedges. Add potato wedges to the bag until 1/3 full. Shake the bag to coat the potatoes. Place them on an oiled pan and repeat until all the potatoes are covered with the mixture. Bake at 350 for 1 hour.

REQUEST

Authors depend on reviews from readers.
If you enjoyed this novella, would you please
consider leaving a review on Amazon?

ABOUT THE AUTHOR

Bestselling and award-winning author Beth Wiseman has sold over two million books. She is the recipient of the coveted Holt Medallion, a two-time Carol Award winner, and she has won the Inspirational Reader's Choice Award three times. Her books have been on various bestseller lists, including the ECPA (Evangelical Christian Publishers Association) and Publishers weekly.

Beth and her husband are empty nesters enjoying country life in south central Texas. Visit her online at BethWiseman.com

ALSO BY BETH WISEMAN

An Amish Bookstore

The Bookseller's Promise

The Story of Love (October 2022)

Hopefully Ever After (Coming soon!)

An Amish Inn

A Picture of Love

An Unlikely Match

A Season of Change

Daughters of the Promise

Plain Perfect

Plain Pursuit

Plain Promise

Plain Paradise

Plain Proposal

Plain Peace

Land of Canaan

Seek Me With All Your Heart

The Wonder of Your Love

His Love Endures Forever

Amish Secrets

Her Brothers Keeper

Love Bears All Things

Home All Along

Amish Journeys

Hearts in Harmony

Listening to Love

A Beautiful Arrangement

Contemporary Women's Fiction

The Promise

A July Bride

The House that Love Built

Need You Now

Surf's Up Series

A Tide Worth Turning

Message In A Bottle

The Shell Collector's Daughter

Christmas by the Sea

Collections

An Amish Christmas Bakery

An Amish Reunion

An Amish Homecoming

An Amish Spring

Amish Celebrations

An Amish Heirloom

An Amish Christmas Love

An Amish Home

An Amish Harvest

An Amish Year

An Amish Cradle

An Amish Second Christmas

An Amish Garden

An Amish Miracle

An Amish Kitchen

An Amish Wedding

An Amish Christmas

Healing Hearts

An Amish Love

An Amish Gathering

Summer Brides

Nonfiction

Writing About The Amish: A Memoir

Children's Book

Saving Angela

Manufactured by Amazon.ca
Bolton, ON

39516829R00066